AWFUL JOURNEY
OF
ONE SIDED LOVE

FANATIXX PUBLICATION
ISO 9001:2015 CERTIFIED

FanatiXx Publication

AM/56, Basanti Colony, Rourkela 769012,
Odisha ISO 9001:2015 CERTIFIED
Website: *www.fanatixx.in*

© Copyright, 2019, Burhanuddin Shayar

All rights reserved. No part of this book may be reproduced, stored in a retrieval system, or transmitted, in any form by any means, electronic, mechanical, magnetic, optical, chemical, manual, photocopying, recording or otherwise, without the prior written consent of its writer.

"Awful Journey of One Sided Love"

By: Burhanuddin Shayar

ISBN: 978-93-89557-33-6

Collection of Poems 1st edition

Book Formatting: Saizal Gupta

Cover Designer: Sagar Samal

The opinions/ contents expressed in this book are solely of the author and do not represent the opinions/ standings/ thoughts of FanatiXx.

ACKNOWLEDGEMENT

For the very first I would like to thank to almighty for all blessings and reason I am here

After almighty I would like to thank my father Mr. Rajabali Shayar for being on my side on every phase of my life and for helping me in my financial sides. Then my mother Mrs. Mubaraka Shayar for always helping me and motivate me in my ups and downs efforts of my life.

I thank my school Madrasah Taiyabiyah and staff and my teachers who nourished me and nurture me in every field and encourage me in my tough times.

I would like to thank all of my family members for trusting me and thank to my entire writer's family who helped me in every phase of my life.

Special thanks to Sakina Khalil and Idris Tapiya for helping me to complete this project.

I thank Phalguni Jagadeesh, Japneet kaur and Ishika Bhardwaj for giving me opportunities.

I thank FanatiXx team for providing this beautiful platform for writers.

Right now whatever I am is because of all the sacrifices of my parents, family and friends.

Thank you all

This book is all about love and showing powerful feelings of unrequited love and other sentimental emotions.

ABOUT THE POET

BURHANUDDIN ABDEALI SHAYAR Born on 08th December 2000. He had studied in Madrasah Taiyebiyah English medium senior secondary school, Partapur. He is doing his graduation from Pune Phuley university. His passion is his dignity. His love towards poems shows his strong feelings, happiness, emotion and strong perfection of virtues. He has achieved many certificates for his success. He still writes, narrates and composes. He had wrote more than four hundred poems and 1 story on one sided love till now. He writes in many languages like Engish, Hindi and Urdu. His write-ups have powerful feeling, love, and other emotions.

The book **"AWFUL JOURNEY OF ONE SIDED LOVE"**
is debut book of his. His extreme interest and a wish for doing something are rushing towards success.

His writings are full of passion of an energy he believes that only very few man are gifted with intellectual faculty that can rise above passion.

CONTENTS

8

POETRY

Someone

The   one
having fun
forge a pun
on someone

Real angle
Truly lovable
Might be amiable
Like to be affable

Our cloy heart
Begin to dart
Undesired to apart
The same as my part
True love
Over and above
Not a shove
But with dove

Heart of someone

Inscribe a ream
On divine dream
Skyscraping esteem
Love is extreme

Heart of someone
Suspicion of someone
Desired destination
Aspire of affiliation

Fabricate a way
Crave to be on way
Just aspire to lay
On pretty heart's tray

Love is outset

Vision blur in love
Posses love in dove
Treating as a friend
Solely ally understand

Actual concern for love
It is a veracious love
Wholly with friend's dove
Not an actual shove

it's all apropos of feeling
Erratically it's killing
With a retort 'NO'
And feeling flow

Goodbye

Every single goodbye
Countenance to die
Preparatory to bye
Goodbye? Why?

Like maltreat in hell
When sayonara tell
Foreboding is not well
Cogent to hot bloody hell

Always covet to let go
Incapable to let go
Waiting for impossible
To crop up confirmable

It is like crucify storm
Alone in bloody storm
Tears will also dry
By insurmountable cry

Someone's beautiful thought
Will miss and yearn a lot
Insomnia and overwrought
Built a big fraught

Presence

Far away
Your way
Beautiful sky
Still on its way

Feel discern sky
Deluge from eye
Cloud of memories
Suffer to die

Hearken the voice
Uplifting voice
Voice of heart beat
Always elite

Love a lot

I don't know love me or not
I don't know accept me or not
I don't know you deserve me or not
I don't know I deserve you or not
I don't know if you trust me or not
I don't know will I ever conquer your trust or not
I don't know if god will fulfill my prayers or not
I don't know whether you will marry me or not
I don't know without you I would be able to live happily
or not
I don't know you will be my life partner or not
I even don't know if my life ends with you or not
But I definitely know
I love you a lot.
A lot.

Promise

I promise you to love you more than myself
I promise you to trust you more than myself
I promise you for being with you till my breath rattle
I promise you to care you more than myself
I promise you to keep you always happy
I promise you to be your side always
I promise you to love only you.

Cutiepie

O sweet cutie pie
Heart is going to tie
Your smile and when cry
I am going to die
Can't evince oodles of
Love to you
The whole shooting match of life
Can't live without you
Only clock ticking in my heart
Nothing without you
One life love life
You are the only life
Love only you
Be creator of life
Accept the pretty love
Convert boring life into wonderful
Show colour of love
Fill in heart
Form it colourful
Can't imagine
Single moment without you

The only and only one
Shape my life joyful
Love and life
be my wife
For Allah's help
Always yelp
Come-on cute pie
On you lemme die

No one left

No one to save
No one is brave
To save you
From plunge brick

Block of feelings
Every time killing
Willing to meet someone
With bricks you dealing

Bricks of thoughts
Make overwrought
Pain of someone like
bricks of bloody thought

Heart dart for someone

Missing part
Can't live apart
Without sweetheart
Heart deny to dart

Thrive with fear and tears
Terrain of pain in vein
Taut from bloody pain
Taunt we wear
Too fear
Tears

Missing someone

Any time with you
Wrapped to see you
Gladness of heart
Frenzied to see you

Only clobber feeling
All time killing
When there is goodbye
All time crying

Hollow in ship of life
Lies in epb tide of life
Missing someone badly
Worst feeling of life

Even don't see you
Even not able to talk you
Even you far away
You are in heart thought
And mind too.

Thoughts of someone

No where left a spot?
Image of someone is not
Find it every where
In heart every time
Every where
I think of heaven
All time 24 x 7
All such holy things
Thought of someone
With wings
Life and way is one
Love's life way to heaven
Love is outset
Someone is angle of heart
Where there is heaven
Missing someone in morning
Thoughts in mind in the evening
And noonly
Love madly
Please come and meet me soon.

Someone special

Whenever we meet someone
Divulge her you are special one
Relate how you love
Never been replaced by anyone

Voice of someone
Crave to hear
Day when perceive her
Is very near
Waiting for that date
O my dear
With tight hug
State you clear
Love you dear

Three magical words
Want them to gird
For only you
Truly, really and madly
Love only you
Angle of my life

Make it bright
Aspire you
You and only you

To see cute face
With big smile on face
Getting mad
To see soon as possible
Eye fills with tear
Cloths of pain we wear
Having bit fear
But try to bear
Tell you love you dear

Precious

Precious for me
Ausoicious for me
Many precious memories
No one dare to stole from me.

Dream girl

Spiel starts with you
Ends with you
All my thoughts
Ends on you
Everything is you
And only you
Only aspire
To live with you
Short time with you
And time without you
Heaven with you
Hell without you
Aspire is to
Share life with you
God knows
I love you
Please shoulder
I can't live without you
Will you marry?
Need to ask you
My heart's beat

Only and only for you

My dream girl is you
My angle is you
My cute pie is you
My someone special is you
Nothing without you
Prayers for you
Aspire is only
To be with you
Love you

Path

Path of love
Lean steps
Power to change
Path of heart is main

Path for me
Your path of me
Allow me
Be there for me

Snags in this path
Obstacle in this path
Barriers and hindrances
Will cross and be on your path

Very end of path
People give last bath
Can't forgot your path
It will very end of my path

Missing heart

Something missing
Its killing
Trying to deal
Heart is only missing

Feel empty
Alone and empty
Loneliness is friend
Now a day's it's a trend

Gifted heart
It is apart
It's an art
Of gift you heart

Love you truly

O lovely heart
Are you apart?
With someone's image
Heart start to dart

Love you truly heart

You are life
Not a rife
Be my wife
O my life

Love you truly my life

The day we met
Can't forgot
Feeling of happiness
The love is outset

Love truly the day we met
Love you truly

Want your heart duly
Aspire to live life
With you fully
I love you truly

Pun

Write some word
Want them to gird
With pain and love
Having vision blurred

Write what I feel
Only for heart appeal
With pain and pen
On paper to heal

Can't bear the pain
Picking up pen
Pain in love
Pain vain

Write about someone
About loved one
Love her the most
And it's done.

Situation

Situations are worst
With voice burst
Only when feel happy
Spoil moments and feel crappy

Happened with me only
Can't get love duly
Don't have better ones
All time lonely

Feel very sad
Am I very bad?
I feel am mad
Eye drops shed

When someone called brother

Epb tide of life
Feeling of disappearance
Want to die
It's not lie
Cry loud
No proud
Tears fell
Not well
Lie on bed
Tears shed
Wipe tears
Lots of fear
Masks have to wear
Fake smile I wear

Why feel crappy when someone tell brother
What happened to son asked mother?
Replied in sad voice nothing my dear
Ammi knows because mother is mother

Stygian night

A lone light
In dark night
Shining moon white
Looks bright
Yearn of procure someone
Life's plight
Someone's image
Looks bright
Single firefly
Teaming in stygian night
Looks like
State of light plight
Single hope
Teaming in dim life
Longing someone in life
Can't endure pain
Missing someone
That someone is who
Make abandonee
Single light
In dark night
Teeming bright

Hope of getting

Someone outright
Lots of pain
In my vein
Pain of missing someone
Swan of someone
Aspire to marry someone

Empty non empty bowl

of heart

Forlorn and empty
In love accidently
Love someone truly
Far flung to feel lonely
Far gone and feel lonely

Desolation of my heart
I can't live apart
Aspire to be a part
My hear dart
With your heart

Love in my heart
Don't tell to depart
Bloody feeling of depart
Man having lion heart
Wanted to be part

Non empty vessel
Without you

Brimful of pain in love
Without you

Getting bore
From core
Totally broken
Without someone

*T*ime

Time is holy thing
Provide two wings
Time heals make you king
Bad time give you sting

Time have two phase
Which make you amaze?
Time is horrible
Time is adorable

Time sometime hurt you
After mutilate will heal you
After hurt there'll help
Exam makes you to yelp
The presence of god
Always with you
After bad there will surely
Some good time for you
Always have faith on almighty Allah
Faith that, that the creator is god
Time goes very fast
Situations are too vast

Painful time
Pace your time
You are in
A Sitch of missing someone
Time slows down
Miss someone
Sorrow and broken
Time of missing someone

Love

Love
I fall
Need your call
Broke all the walls
Please make me your thrall
Love you only you
Aspire are you
Missing you
You

Two body one soul

Two bodies
One soul
Future goal
Far away
Found my soul
On your way
Let's go for date
Please don't get late
I feel saudade
When you are late
Always pray for
Future with you
Want to share
Future with you
Want to have
Trip with you
May Allah
Keep with you
You are far

Feel your soul
Unaccompanied by you
Heart is an empty bowl
But heart fills with pain

Called it as unkempt
Unkempt bowl of pain
Without you
Feel great pain
Miss you again and again
Feel love in vein
But with me
Have to take brain
Let's begin new life
But please don't rife
Want you to be in life
Want only you it's not rife

In melle

Every second I passed
Brain asked
What are you doing?
I am missing

Missing what?
Missing someone in rut
What? You got mad
In love vision fade

Going on wrong way
On my loves way
Love someone earnestly
Missing someone honestly
From first light
Light at night
Feeling of someone
Always bite

Every of hours
And after hours
Pain remains

In every hour

Can't endure pain
Pain in every vein
With you in a while
Pain will vain

When get someone
Pain will wane
When get loved
Then only get dove

Dove is
Emblem of peace
I will got it
When pain release

Will get
My heart piece
Only mine
Aspire and caprice

That date

That is the time of first date
Want to do something special on that date
Successfully met each other at last
Be there before five minute and I wait

Join me
Sit near me
Her smile to feel blessed
Order glass of slush for me

No topic to share
Looked at her and stare
At public place
Stare and don't care
Garden of love
Near place we met
Sit together
Aspire to live together
Open gift
Open with sift
Wow it's too nice
This is concise

Thoughts

In Utmost Thought
Miss You A Lot
Absence Forge Distraught
Accompanied Overwrought

Feel You in Arms
You Sweet Cute Charm
Draw Breath With
It's Not Myth

Thoughts of Love
Make Me Happy
YOUR ABSENCE
MAKE CRAPPY

Hunch of Losing You
Please Give Some Clue
Clue You Also Love Me
Pledge You Live With Me

Postulation of Getting You
Love Is Always True
Come and Take a View
View of Love for You

You Are Far Away
To Talk There Is No Way
Your Thoughts on Way
Always Be There On Way

Some Times Give Happiness
Sometime Sadness
Madness for Someone
Stole Wellness

Thoughts of You
Make Happy
Thoughts Losing You
Make Crappy

Alive

Trust on almighty Allah
Make me to alive
Am honey bee
You are hive
Without home
One cannot live
Hope of getting you
Help me to revive
If am fish
You are water
Am rainbow
You are color
Without water
Fist cannot live
Without you can't be alive

If am pen
You are ink
No use of pen
With an empty ink
Am pencil
You are lid

Without you
Am dead
Am human
You are good deeds
Difference only of good deeds
You can make alive
Without you
Cant able to revive

Pain

How to endure pain
How to handle in vein
In every vein
Feel you and lots of pain
Hear you but mentally
Far away physically
Want you
Physically as well mentally
Want you
Bodily
Always in search
To get your love
I lurch
Aspire to get
Love with dove
Want to win you
And your love
Cry loud for getting you
Instead of searching you
Am vagabond searching for you love
Your love when and where

When you are not with
Feel that heart is not with
Heart remains with you
How get back as you.

Keychain

Heart shaped keychain
Her name in vein
Heart restrains words
Like all them to gird

For key of success
Kitchen for her success
With chain named friends
For key of new trends

Start with word friends
Love you with eye blind
Happiness to give you
Memories with you

Your named keychain
Written on every vein
In heart and even in
Small brain

Rut your cute name
And all pain wane

Pitch in your nature
Show your signature

Word of seven letters
Life sweet and better
Probing for nectar
There's bee like nectar

Queen's crown

Pearls of love
Showing dove
With cute flower
Faux rose flower

Pretty crown
On hair brown
Bonny round
Make it down

With friend
Not a trend
It is amend
After attend

Watch

Time is important
You are too important
Gifted pretty watch
Wrist cute watch

Time spent together
Place and talks gathers
Planned meet
Love that meet

Appeal allow to meet
Your place moment we met
Offers glass of juice
Gifted watch and love induced

Two chairs
Show care
Love your hair
Aspire to be pair

See your face
Reflect happiness

See you happy
Feel happiness

Helps to see time
Want you to be mine
Always pray Allah
To make you mine

Way of love

You are far away
But its way
Never forget you
I feel you every day
Always when I lay
At night and day
Only one way

Text

Only one text
Want your text
Salutary text says well
Make my day
In good mood
But ignores me
Your ignorance and I die
Forgot to smile
Forgot how to be happy
Forgot how to laugh
Forgot my charm
Forgot everything
But never forget you
You are always with me
Pain from your side
Accept it and keep with me
What is happiness?
Forgot to be happy
Adopted to be sad
Always feel sadness
Why can't feel happiness

Why feels crappiness
Become crappy in love
Need some love?
And dove
To make life happy again
You have to love
Love you a lot
Want always you to be happy

Hurt and hate

Waiting since many days
For only one day
But your reply says
no not me go away
Is this good
Feeling for love
Not get love
Get hurt
Hurt and hate
But love or hate
Love you mate
Don't get late

Prayer

Prayer
Not always
Prayer works
Sometime no ways
Only says
Go away
Don't use
Don't refuse
Feeling loose
Just choose
Wait only
My wait
You late
Wait not late
Only I wait
Awful night
With moon bright
No light
No stars flight
Only white moon
And its light

For you I shout
Cry loud
No doubt
Feeling out.

Rain of pain

There   always pain
Which want to wane?
Like heavy rain
Rain of pain remain

Pain always fall on
Rain also fall on
Love dove is an umbrella
Let's walk under umbrella

Umbrella of love
Provide dove
At time of pain
And pain wane

Umbrella help from rain
Love care help from pain
With lots of love pain will wane
With dove and care pain wane

Let's show love
Make some dove

Just be a beloved
Just make dove

Don't shove into pain
Don't shove into rain
That is the Rain of pain
Which will never wane?

Let's show care
Let's do prayer
Let make it need
Let them feed

Let's them help
Who always yelp?
For getting love
Give them dove

Distance from my heart

My heart with you
Which is asked?
In love with you
I had gifted you.

Without you I cry
Without you I awry
My cry with your bye
Again your absence why?

From me you are far away
And my cry I can't allay
Bloody nights and days
Without you there's no way

I am like heartless guy
When you say me bye
With you my heart says bye
And my eyes start to cry

Want you beside me
My heart in you but with me

Together forever only with me
Yes, I want your heart with me

Why you say goodbye
Why you leave me to die
Why you are so far away
I feel saudade and I cry

Qayamat   For me your absence
Far away from you my distance
Without you I feel totally imbalance
Why there always you outdistance

My lots of love with you
But existence not with you
Yes, I gift my heart to you
Take my heart always with you

Live life fully

Look at sky
Don't say why?
Sky of success
By saying why?
Please don't die
Success you tie
Knot it with life
Humanity you buy
Together you live
Love you give
Please show care
Clothes you wear
Is of generosity
And also integrity
Clothes you tear
It's of evil and fear
Evil of backbiting
And complaining

Evil of lie
Will let you die
So don't die
Live life fully
I said it truly.

Fear

Don't Don't fear
O my dear
Pain u bear
Just a fear

Forgot your pain
Yes, it's an arcane
You have to learn
Confidence you earn

Stood strong
Live lifelong
With no fear
Pain you bear

Bear your fear
It's simply clear
Do everything
You can't bear

Confidence is your friend
And Fear is only an end
Stop ending be a trend
Please don't depend

Cast you toward fear
Don't fear of tears
Just Jeer on your fear
Wipe away your tear

Try to conquer
Be an adventurer
Control your fear
Enjoy life and cheer

Try and cry

Yes, I am trying
But from inside
I am dying
I can't express that feeling
I always hide
Like feelings died

I don't want to win
But I am trying to win
That situation
And my agitation
I can't explain in words
Pain that I can't gird

Really don't want to try but trying
Looks I don't want to die but dying
Trying crying denying and doing
And yes I don't want but I am winning
But in this, special one I am loosing
Race I will win but someone I am loosing

Late reply

Those days
Miss everyday
When you reply in seconds
But nowadays
Blue tick remains
No reply no text
From many days
Anyways
When my life ends
You find my way
Miss and hiss
And beautiful days

Book of my life ends

Cute life
Just a rife
Big strife
Want afterlife

When life ends
Want you best friend
Not want end
But have to attend

Attend areal
Almighty's angel
Heaven and hell
Not to yell

Yell for you
Want you to glue
Don't skew
Just want you

The day of judgement

You will say when I die
You will cry
Surely miss
And then hiss

You will miss me
And then hiss for me
Try not to miss
But surely you hiss

Miss my act
Jokes I cracked
How you react
Bangles you will wrack

That day

I love you
But not here to listen you

nd

Till the very end
When death is appended
I can't imagine my life
Without you is only strife
You are my best friend
On you I am depend
Need you yes you afterlife
Afterlife is not rife
You are beautiful chapter
And you are like captor
Capture my heart
Without you can't dart
Without dart will die
Without you surely die
Don't take light it's not lie
I will die without you
My love towards you is askew

You may contact the Publisher at:

www.fanatixx.in

www.ingramcontent.com/pod-product-compliance
Lightning Source LLC
Chambersburg PA
CBHW051452140726
47987CB00006B/2674